For Jonathan, who always leaves early—K. E.

For Hannah and Evan—D. Y.

A FEIWEL AND FRIENDS BOOK
An Imprint of Macmillan

 Printed in China by South China Printing Co. Ltd., Dongguan City, Guangdong Province.
For information, address Feiwel and Friends, 175 Fifth Avenue, New York, N.Y. 10010.

Library of Congress Cataloging-in-Publication Data Available

ISBN: 978-1-250-00080-4

The art was created with gouache
on watercolor paper.

Book design by Katie Cline

Feiwel and Friends logo designed by Filomena Tuosto

First Edition: 2012

10 9 8 7 6 5 4 3 2 1

mackids.com

KATE AND NATE ARE RUNNING LATE!

by Kate Egan • illustrated by Dan Yaccarino

FEIWEL AND FRIENDS
NEW YORK

Nate creeps into the darkened room.
His mom is sound asleep.
First he shakes her, tries to wake her.
Then he takes a flying leap!

MADDIE
NATE

"It's getting late," announces Nate.
Kate rolls over, rubs her eyes.
She sits up straight. "Oh, that's just great.
Not again!" Nate's mother sighs.

Nate has preschool in the morning,
aftercare all afternoon.
Like every day, they have to rush.
Kate's day at work starts soon.

Kate yells, "Time to use the potty!"
when she's halfway down the stairs.

She starts the coffee, feeds the cats,
toasts some waffles, slices pears.

Nate's not happy, nor is Maddie.
(That's his sister—she is eight.)
They hate to rush, they hate to hurry,
but there's no time to hesitate.

"I think we'll make it," Kate tells Nate.
"Please get dressed and brush your teeth."

Nate's not hearing, only playing.
"Time to move!" says Kate. "Good grief!"

Nate eats his breakfast,
clears his plate,
drinks some juice,
and makes his bed.

Kate's in the shower for an hour,
(so it seems 'cause Nate's ahead).

"Where's my homework?" Maddie grumbles.
"Someone took it. Maybe you?"
Nate's big sister finds her folder.
But her socks? She has no clue.

**They're almost ready, feeling steady,
wearing coats and big backpacks.
They have mittens, boots, and lunches,
water bottles, healthy snacks.**

Then there's trouble on the double.
Cats run out the open door.

Maddie gets them, then she pets them.
Now, they're later than before!

Nate says, "Wait! I need my bunny!"
Kate regards him with dismay.

"Just one minute, I'll be speedy. . . ."
Kate gives up. "That's fine, okay."

**Nate races off at lightning speed.
He doesn't see the puddle.
There's ice on top and Nate can't stop.
So now, they're in a muddle.**

Nate falls in backward, landing hard.
Now, he's wet! Tears start to flow.

**Kate kisses him and calms him down.
Even so, it's time to go!**

"There's been a change in plans," says Kate.
"We need to drive instead of walk."

The kids climb in, they buckle up.
Their mom's too tense to talk.

They squeal down streets, they round a bend.
Traffic's light, it seems to Kate.
"Where's everyone?" she wonders.
Then, "Has anyone checked the date?"

The schoolyard's empty, nothing doing.
No one's lined up, not today.

No one's playing, no one's staying.
That's because it's Saturday!